24. AUG 12.

06. APR 1&

13. JUL 13.

19. AUG 13.

KT-398-558

Get **more** out of libraries

Please return or renew this item by the last date shown.

You can renew online at www.hants.gov.uk/library

Or by phoning 0845 603 5631

Hampshire
County Council

Sue Graves

W

A story in a familiar setting

First published in 2011 by
Franklin Watts
338 Euston Road
London NW1 3BH

Franklin Watts Australia
Level 17/207 Kent Street
Sydney NSW 2000

A CIP catalogue record for this book is
available from the British Library.

ISBN: 978 1 4451 0407 2 (hbk)
ISBN: 978 1 4451 0415 7 (pbk)

Illustrations by Artful Doodlers Ltd.
Art Director: Jonathan Hair
Series Editor: Jackie Hamley
Series Designer: Matthew Lilly

Printed in China

Franklin Watts is a division of
Hachette Children's Books,
an Hachette UK company
www.hachette.co.uk

Kim, Sal and Ash
were at the seaside.

Scully and Scrap
were with them.

They all went up
on the rocks.

Ash saw a cave in the rocks.
"Let's go in the cave!" he said.
"It will be fun!"

"I don't like caves," said Kim.
"Caves are damp and dark.
I bet cave monsters live
in damp, dark caves."
"There are no monsters,"
said Sal. "Come on!"

The cave was very dark.
It was very damp, too.
Kim was scared.
"I don't like this cave,"
he said. "Let's go!"

Suddenly, Ash saw
some shadows.
He was scared, too.
"Look!" he said. "There **are**
monsters in this cave!"

Ash hid behind Kim.
The shadows got bigger.
They came closer.

Sal was scared.
"There are big monsters
in this cave!" she said.
Sal hid behind Ash.

The shadows got bigger and bigger. They came closer and closer. Sal and Ash ran and hid behind a big rock.

"Woof! Woof!" said one shadow.

22

Woof!
Woof!

"Yap! Yap!" said the other shadow. "Cave monsters don't woof and yap," said Kim.

Kim took a closer look. Then he laughed and laughed! "There are no monsters in the cave at all!" he said. "Look!"

Puzzles

Which speech bubbles belong to Ash?

Which words describe Kim
at the start of the story and which
describe him at the end?

frightened

delighted

happy

nervous

scared

thrilled

Answers

Ash's speech bubbles are: 1, 4

At the start of the story, Kim is:
frightened, nervous, scared.
At the end of the story, Kim is:
delighted, happy, thrilled.

Espresso Connections

This book may be used in conjunction with the Science area on Espresso to introduce topics on light and shadows.

It may also be used in conjunction with the Geography area for creative writing activities. Here are some suggestions.

Light and Shadows

Visit "Light and Dark" in Science 1. Play the children the video "What are Shadows?"

Discuss the question at the end: What would happen if a cloud came out and blocked the sunlight?

Then watch the video "Making Shadows". Talk further about how light travels and how an object must be blocking the light to make a shadow.

Ask children to work in a group and draw the cave where Kim, Sal and Ash are exploring. Ask them to mark where the back of the cave is, where the light is coming from, and where Scully and Scrap must be to make the shadows on the wall.

Visit The Activities section and play the "Shadow memory game".

Write your own concrete poem / Design your own poster

Visit the "Journey to the coast" in Geography 1, and go to the Activity arcade.

Choose "Concrete poetry". Write some concrete poems about the seaside and print them out.

Choose "Poster designer" Design some class posters encouraging poeple to visit the seaside. Try to use some of the seaside vocabulary you used to write your concrete poems.